THE TEACHINGS OF DEVKI PUTRA

SUBH CHATTERJEE

Contents

Preface

The main theme of the Mahabharata is the idea of sacred duty. Every character in the epic is born into a particular social group, or caste, that must follow the duty prescribed to it by sacred law. The characters who perform their sacred duty are rewarded, while those who do not are punished.

About The Author

Subh Chatterjee

Thanks for reading this book. Hope you all like the work. This book has been written by me. But the words here are told by Lord Shree Krishna. In the Gita, a Pandava brother Arjuna loses his will to fight and has a discussion with his charioteer Krishna, about duty, action, and renunciation. The Gita has three major themes: knowledge, action, and love.

The two armies had gathered on the battlefield of Kurukshetra, well prepared to fight a war that was inevitable. Still, in this verse, King Dhritarashtra asked Sanjay, what his sons and his brother Pandu's sons were doing on the battlefield? It was apparent that they Would fight, then why did he ask such a question The blind King Dhritarashtra's fondness for his own sons had clouded his spiritual wisdom and deviated

him from the path of virtue. He had usurped the kingdom of Hastinapur from the rightful heirs; the Pandavas, sons of his brother Pandu. Feeling guilty of the injustice he had done towards his nephews, his conscience worried him about the outcome of this battle.

CHAPTER TWO

Sanjay understood Dhritarashtra's concern, who wanted an assurance that the battle would eventuate. Sanjay tried to allay his worry by informing that the Pandava army was standing in a military formation, ready for battle. Then he moved on to tell him what his son Duryodhana was doing on the battlefield

As King Dhritarashtra was blind, his eldest son Duryodhana virtually ruled the kingdom of Hastinapur. In the Mahabharata, he is described as very rude, egoistic, evil and cruel by nature. Since his childhood, he had a strong dislike for the Pandavas and left no opportunity to demean them. He was aware that to

rule over the entire kingdom of Hastinapur unchallenged he needed to eliminate them. However, standing on the battlefield, when he saw the large Pandava army, he was baffled. He had underestimated the Pandavas, the extent of military might they had gathered was way beyond his expectation.

CHAPTER THREE

Duryodhana asked Dronacharya to look at the skillfully arranged military phalanx of the Pandava army led by their commander-in-chief Dhristadyumna, King Dhrupad's son. He was also one of Dronacharya's pupils. Duryodhana was subtly reminding his teacher of a mistake he had committed in the past.

Many years back, Dronacharya along with the Pandavas had defeated King Drupad in a battle and took away half his kingdom. To avenge his defeat, Drupad performed a sacrifice to beget a son. Dhristadyumna was born out of that sacrificial fire, with a boon that he would kill Dronacharya in the future. Even though Dronacharya was aware, when he was approached for Dhristadyumna's military training, he very humbly accepted and imparted all his knowledge impartialy to his pupil. Duryodhana was reminding Dronacharya that even though Dhristadyumna was his pupil, he was also Drupad's son, with a boon to kill him. He wanted to ensure that as in the past, Dhronacharya should not become lenient towards his pupils, now that, they were oon the battlefield.

CHAPTER FOUR

Due to his anxiety, the Pandava army seemed much larger to Duryodhan than it actually was. He had
never expected his opponents would mobilize an army of warriorS with such military prowess, who would be formidable in battle. Out of fear of the looming catastrophe, he started enumerating the names of all the mahārathīs (warriors who were singly equivalent in strength to ten thousand ordinary warriors) gathered on the Pandava side. They were all exceptional heroes, and great military commanders, equivalent in valor to his cousins Arjun and Bheem.

CHAPTER FIVE

Dronacharya was a teacher of military science and not really a warrior. However, he was on the battlefield as one of the commanders of the Kaurava army. An impudent Duryodhanam even doubted the loyalty of his own preceptor. Cunning Duryodhana purposefully addressed his teacher as dwijottama (best amongst the twice-born, or Brahmins). His denigrating and vailed reminder for Dronacharya was that, if he did not display his valor in this battle, he would be considered a lowly Brahmin, who was only interested in the
fine food and lavish lifestyle at the king's palace. Then to cover up his vicious words and boost his teacher's
and his own morale; Duryodhana started naming all the great generals present on the Kaurava side, describing their valor and military expertise.

CHAPTER SIX

The commander-in-chief of the Kaurava army was Grandsire Bheeshma. Apart from being an exceptional warrior, he had an extraordinary boon. He could choose the time of his death, this meant he was practically invincible. Duryodhana felt that under Bheeshma's command their army was undefeatable. Whereas, the Pandava army was secured by Duryodhana's sworn enemy, Bheema. Hence, he started comparing his Grandfather Bheeshma's strength with his cousin Bheema.

Vinaash kale vipreet buddhi as the proverb goes, which means that when the end draws near, egoistic people indulge in vainglory instead of being humble in evaluating their situation. This tragic irony of fate is reflected here in Duryodhana's self-aggrandizing statement that; their army's strength secured by

Bheeshma was unlimited.

However, both Kauravas and Pandavas were Bheeshma's grandchildren and as the oldest living member of the Kuru family, he was concerned about their welfare. He was compassionate towards the Pandavas, but was bound by his ethical commitment towards the throne of Hastinapur and its subjects.

Therefore, halfheartedly, he led the Kaurava army against them. Bheeshma was also aware that in this holy war, along with all the great warriors of the world the Supreme Lord Krishna Himself was present. Lord Krishna was with the

Pandavas, which meant Dharma was on their side, and no power in thee entire universe could make the side of Adharma win. He had vowed to protect the kingdom of Hastinapur and its subjects and to fulfill his responsibility towards them Bheeshma led the Kaurava army, even though he was aware of their wrongdoings. This decision of Bheeshma acocentuates his strength of character and enigmatic personality.

CHAPTER SEVEN

Duryodhana urged all the Kaurava generals to make sure they are around Grandsire Bheeshma and give him full support while they defend their own respective positions in the military phalanx. Duryodhana beheld Bheeshma's unassailability as an advantage and wanted to use it as strength and inspiration for his army.

CHAPTER EIGHT

Bheeshma was aware that Duryodhana had no chance of victory as the Supreme Lord Shree Krishna was on the opposite side. However, he understood his grand-nephew's anxiety and to cheer him up he blew his
conch shell loudly. In olden days, blowing of the conch shell in the battlefield signaled the start of the war. This also conveyed to Duryodhana that Bheeshma was ready to lead the Kaurava army and he would fight dutifully and spare no pain.

CHAPTER NINE

On hearing Bheeshma's call for battle, everyone in the Kaurava army also started playing various instruments eagerly, creating tumultuous sound. Shaṅkhāh means conches, panav are drums, ānak kettledrums, bhreyah bugles, and go-mukh are blowing horns. Al these instruments playing together created a loud pandemonium.

CHAPTER TEN

The uproar of the Kaurava army had started to wane. Then from the Pandava side, seated on a magnificent chariot the Supreme Lord Shree Krishna and Arjun, both blew their conch shells intrepidly, which ignited the enthusiasm of the Pandava army as well. Here, Sanjay has addressed Lord Shree Krishna as "Madhav". It is a combination of two words, Mā which refers to goddess Lakshmi, the goddess of prosperity and dhav is used for husband. Goddess Lakshmim is Lord Vishnu's wife, who is one of the many forms of Shree Krishna. This verse implies that the goddess of prosperity was with the Pandavas, and by her grace, they would be triumphant in this war and reclaim their kingdom soon. The sons of King Pandu are called Pandavas and it may be used for any of the five brothers. In this verse, the Pandava being referred to is Arjun, the thirad among the five. He was a mighty warrior and a superior archer. His magnificent chariot was a gift from Agni, the celestial god of fire.

In this verse, Shree Krishna is addressed as "Hrishikesh" which means the Lord of the mind and senses. Shree Krishna is the Sovereign Master of everybody's minds and senses. Throughout his wonderful pastimes, he displayed complete control over his mind and senses.

CHAPTER TWELVE

Yudhisthtira, the eldest Pandava is being addressed here as "King." He always displayed royal grace and nobility, whether living in a palace or in a forest when in exile. He also got this title by performing the Rājasūya Yajña a royal sacrifice, which earned him tributes from all the other kings of the world. In this verse, Sanjay also called Dhritarashtra the "Ruler of the earth." The real reason for this appellation was to remind him of his duties as the ruler of the country. With so many kings and princes participating from both sides in this war, it was as if the entire earth was split into two parties. It was definite that this

mammoth war Would cause irreversible destruction. The only person who could stop the war at this juncture was Dhritarashtra, and Sanjay wanted to know if he was willing to do that.

CHAPTER THIRTEEN

Sanjay conveyed to Dhritarashtra, that the tremendous sound of the various conch shells from the Pandava army was shattering the hearts of his sons. Whereas, he did not mention any such reaction from the Pandavas, when the Kauravas were creating a commotion. The Kauravas were fearful, as their conscience pricked them for their crimes and misdeeds. They were relying solely on their physical strength to fight the
war. However, the Pandavas were confident and felt protected, as the Supreme Lord Shree Krishna was by their side, their victory was definite.

CHAPTER FOURTEEN

Here Sanjay addresses Arjun by another name, "Kapi Dhwaj," which means "Monkey Bannered." This denotes the presence of the mighty Monkey God; Hanuman on Arjun's chariot. It so happened that, once

Arjun became very boastful of his archery skills and quipped at Shree Krishna. He said, "I do not understand why during Lord Rama's tinme, the monkeys worked so hard to make a bridge from India to Lanka with heavy stones? If I was there, I would have made a bridge of arrows." The Omniscient Lord asked him, "Alright, go ahead show me your bridge" Very skillfully Arjun showered thousands of arrows and made a huge bridge. Now, it was time to test it. Shree Krishna called upon great Hanuman for the job. As soon as Hanuman started walking on the bridge, it started crumbling under his feet. Arjun realized his folly; his bridge of arrows could not have upheld the weight of Lord Rama's huge army. He asked for their forgiveness. Subsequently, Hanuman gave Arjun lessons on being humble and never be proud of his skills.

He also granted Arjun a boon that, during the great war, he would seat himself on Arjun's chariot. Therefore, Arjun's chariot flag carried the insignia of the great Hanuman.

CHAPTER FIFTEEN

Arjun was a skilled warrior, and the most powerful Hanuman was sitting on top of his magnificent chariot. Moreover, his devotion towards the Supreme Lord Shree Krishna was such that, the Lord himself had agreed to be Arjun's charioteer. Here, Arjun was seated on the passenger seat giving instructions to Shree Krishna, his charioteer. He addresses the Lord as Achyuta, the most dependable One and requests him to place the chariot in the middle of the battlefield. "Although I am Supremely Independent, yet I become enslaved by My devotees. They are very dear to Me, and I become indebted to them for their love." Such is the beauty of God's bond with his devotees that He gets enslaved, beholden by His devotees' love.

CHAPTER SIXTEEN

Arjun was fearless, the Supreme Lord was his charioteer. His outlook was that the Pandavas were legitimately entitled to half the kingdom of Hastinapur, but the wicked sons of Dhritarashtra, the Kauravas had not agreed to share. Arjun was ready for battle, eager to get back what was rightfully theirs and punish them for all their past wrongdoings. His request for the chariot to be placed in the middle of the battlefield was to take a closer look at the Kaurava army. Arjun wanted to see all those who had taken the side of injustice. He wanted to punish them equally, as they had chosen to be on the wrong side, none of them would be spared.

CHAPTER SEVENTEEN

Here, Dhritarashtra is being addressed as Bhārata by Sanjay, which means, "O descendant of the great King Bharat..

CHAPTER EIGHTEEN

Shree Krishna called Arjun "Parth, son of Pritha, another name for his mother Kunti." Then he pointed at all the warriors like Bhishma, Drona and other kings on the Kaurava side and deliberately used the word "Kuru" to address them. It was to remind Arjun that both Kauravas and Pandavas were all decedents of the great king Kuru. Therefore, the enemy he wasso eager to kill was actually his own family and relatives. The
Omniscient Lord was sowing the seed of delusion in Arjun's mind, only to eliminate it later. He was preparing the ground for the gospel he was about to preach The Bhagavad Geeta, which would benefit the future generations in the age of Kali.

CHAPTER NINETEEN

Shree Krishna's words had the desired effect on Arjun. Looking at the armies on both sides of the battlefield, his heart sank, they were all "Kurus" his relatives. The brave warrior who wanted to punish the Kauravas for all their wickedness a few minutes back suddenly became fearful. Comprehending the devastation this war would cause, his valor started to diminish. Hence, Sanjay has called him Kaunteyah the son of Kunti, denoting that Arjun had become softhearted, similar to his mother. However, Arjun was now very confused and his mind filled with questions.

CHAPTER TWENTY

Arjun realized that all the warriors on the battlefield ready to shed blood were none other than his own relatives, friends, and family. He was filled with remorse and fearful of performing his duty of fighting this war. The cause for these sentiments was his attachment towards his bodily relatives. He became forgetful of his spiritual existence, that he was not just the body. His affection for his bodily relatives had blinded his consciousness. In the materialistic concept, we consider ourselves to be only the body, which is emotionally attached to all its bodily relatives. As this attachment is based on ignorance it carries with it the physical burdens of life like pain, sorrow, grief, and death. Only the death of the physical body can end these materialistic attachments. We are more than just the physical body; our eternal souls are beyond life and death. Tangled in the various attachments of the material world, we keep forgetting that the Supreme Lord is our only permanent relative. He is the Father, Mother, Friend, Master, and Beloved of our soul.

CHAPTER TWENTY-ONE

Here Arjun has addressed Shree Krishna as Keśhava, killer of a demon called Keshi. Yet, for Arjun the thought of killing his own relatives troubled him to such an extent that, his body started to tremble. He was unable to even hold his magnificent bow Gāṇdīv, which could emit sounds that petrified even the most powerful enemies. Arjun had become so disillusioned that superstition started gripping him. He could only see bad omens indicating severe devastation. Thus, he felt it would be a sin to engage in such a battle.

CHAPTER TWENTY-TWO

Taking away someone's life itself is immoral, and killing a relative is considered even more sinful. Arjun was in a dilemma, what would he gain with victory achieved by such a heinous act? It would not give him any joy; as he would have lost all the people who mattered to him. Detachment to worldly assets is a commendable virtue. Even though Arjun's thoughts were moral and virtuous, they were not spiritual sentiments. They were budding out of compassion and attachment towards his relatives. Spiritual sentiments bestow peace, harmony, and happiness to a soul. However, Arjun's situation was not such he was disillusioned, confused, and losing control over his body and mind.